Knowledge Workings Thea
produced Alms in May of
TheaterLab in New Yor

John Clay -- Director

Marjorie Phillips Elliott -- Executive
Producer

Cast

Brian McKenzie - Aaron Long

Sister Catherine Imelda - Kathleen
Huber

Martin Mahoney - Jack Farrell

CHARACTERS

Brian McKenzie, an enthusiastic Midnight Run volunteer in his thirties

Sister Catherine Imelda, a seventy-seven-year-old nun in charge of the Midnight Run

Martin Mahoney, a 'retired' sportswriter in his sixties

[NOTE: dialogue ending with this symbol '...//' indicates that the next character speaking overlaps that line in their reply.]

A church basement with two tables and entrances both stage right and stage left. The former leads to the stairs to the church proper. The latter leads to its parking lot. Some janitorial tool —a broom, a bucket, some rags —lean against the wall stage left.

Early April, 9pm, the day before Palm Sunday

ALMS

A Play in One Act

By

T.J. Elliott and Joe Queenan

https://offthewallplays.com

BRIAN, in his mid-30s, dressed in well-appointed business-casual attire, stands stage right at a table assembling toiletry bags. He is a model of assembly-line efficiency, lining up the different types of small bottles, and then moving them into plastic baggies. He meticulously Ziplocs each bag prior to placing it carefully in the box on the floor. SISTER CATHERINE IMELDA enters from stage right, tall and erect despite being in her mid-to-late 70s, wearing severe eyeglasses and a modern habit.

SISTER
CATHERINE
IMELDA

Are we forsaken tonight?
Utterly forsaken?

BRIAN

Sometimes they come late,
Sister.

SISTER
CATHERINE
IMELDA

(*Nodding*) The Good Lord
will provide. He always
does.

She exits, and BRIAN continues his efficient operation. MARTIN, in his sixties, dressed in faded jeans and a sweatshirt, enters from stage left with a well-stuffed black garbage bag filled with unsorted toiletries of the type provided by hotel chains.

                    MARTIN

Hey.

                    BRIAN

(*Overly enthusiastic*) Good evening!

                    MARTIN

Is this where this goes?

                    BRIAN

Toiletries or food?

                    MARTIN

Toiletries. Tons of them. My wife collects them when she's on the road.

                    BRIAN

Nice! We sure can use them.

                    MARTIN

So, where do you want them?

                       BRIAN

          In the baggies. Like this.

Holds up one of the Ziploc bags.

                       MARTIN

          Rita said it was just in and
          out.

                       BRIAN

          Right. But the bottles still
          need to be sorted into
          individual kits.

*With one hand, he points to a poster behind
him that shows the various steps comprising
the kit assembly, and with the other holds up
a baggie.*

          You know—for the Midnight
          Run.

                    *MARTIN looks
                    confused.*

          The Mission of Mercy for the
          Homeless?

Back to bagging while MARTIN watches.

                       MARTIN

          That looks pretty
          complicated.

                       BRIAN

          It's easier to hand out as an
          individualized packet.

MARTIN

Individualized.

Nods his head.

And where do they go
before someone puts them
in the baggies, according to
the official Catholic Boy
Scout manual up there?

BRIAN

That table is fine.

*Goes back to his assembling. MARTIN
observes him for a moment.*

MARTIN

Are you the only one
packing?

BRIAN

There's Sister, but she's
mostly supervising.

Looks at his watch.

Oh, boy. Running out of
time.

Points to MARTIN's bag.

Oh, I should get your name.

*Grabs a pen and a clipboard and moves over
to shake MARTIN's hand.*

I'm Brian McKenzie.

Warily, MARTIN shakes his hand.

MARTIN

Martin. Martin Mahoney.

BRIAN writes this down.

My wife is really the donor.
Rita. Make sure she gets the
credit. She's saving up for a
plenary indulgence. This
delivery might put her over
the top.

BRIAN

A what?

MARTIN

A plenary indulgence.

BRIAN

Is that some kind of tax
deduction thing?

MARTIN

A plenary indulgence. Come
on.

Rattles off the definition rapidly.

A remission before God of
the temporal punishment
due to sins whose guilt has
already been forgiven.

BRIAN

(Suddenly recognizing the term.) Oh, right. Indulgences. Martin Luther. John Tetzel. *(Grimaces.)* I'm studying that in church history but *(Gestures.)* I didn't make the connection. *(Beat.)* You were joking.

MARTIN

Don't tell my wife that.

BRIAN

Puzzled and smiling.

Over my head. Sorry, we're driving down to the South Bronx tonight.

Enthusiastic.

Sister says the Bronx is the poorest part of New York.

MARTIN

I grew up there. The blight at the end of the tunnel.

BRIAN

Really? You lived in the Bronx?

MARTIN

Somebody had to...

BRIAN

Sister taught there! She retired here but keeps on going back with the "Run". I think it's because The Bronx has the most homeless.

MARTIN

Everyone's good at something. Even da Bronx.

BRIAN

(Rambling) Sister has us go under the bridges, out into the pocket parks. People come out like some sort of zombie movie. Not that they are zombies; the poor are *definitely* still human beings. (*Looks at watch again*) Oh boy, gotta pick up the pace here. Sister will...//

MARTIN

Wallop you with the steel ruler?

BRIAN looks very puzzled.

BRIAN

No. When I said–I just meant
Sister will be disappointed if
we're late. She runs a tight
ship around here.

MARTIN

And you're the sole
swabbie?

BRIAN

(*Talking while filling bags*)
Well, so far tonight. But
generally, we get a good
little group in here. The
Devlins. Frank DeLuis brings
his son Michael.

*Blank-faced, MARTIN does not recognize
these names.*

He's a deacon. Tom and
Eileen Landers? They're all
Run regulars. You know
them?

MARTIN

I'm more of a Dawn Patrol
kind of guy.

BRIAN

Do you belong to Saint
Aquinas?

MARTIN

Nah, I'm more of an episodic
Catholic. Binge at Christmas
and Easter. Hit the ashes on
Ash Wednesday, Holy Hour
on Good Friday. Midnight
mass, at least through the
Carols. And then I dry out
until my next spiritual
bender.

BRIAN looks attentive, like he is trying to
understand all of this, but is very puzzled and
it shows.

MARTIN stays deadpan as BRIAN studies his
face.

BRIAN

I should really get back to
this. (*Overly solicitous*) Sister
tells people to drop off the
stuff in packets. Gave out the
flyer after all the masses last
week. *(With emphasis)* By
herself. Standing there from
seven AM until one PM.
She's amazing. But it's all
good. I get it, you didn't see
the flyer.

MARTIN

(*Looks at his watch*) I'm
pretty sure that it's not all
good right now and that it is
rarely, if ever, all good. But
I'll give you a hand.

He grabs a box of baggies from BRIAN's table and walks back over to the other table, where he dumps out the contents of his large black plastic garbage bag.

                    BRIAN

          You are a godsend. Thanks
          so much, Martin. The rules
          are up there.

Again, points to the poster.

                    MARTIN

          The rules. Canon law even
          extends to this? (*Reads*)
          Shampoo, conditioner, soap,
          toothpaste, toothbrush.
          Hang on a second—no night
          cream? No clay mask? No
          exfoliating lotion?

                    BRIAN

          (*Confused for a moment*) Ha.
          No. Just the basics. But
          sorted, like it says. (*Points to
          the poster*) And we do snack
          packs too.

                    MARTIN

          Anything tasty?

BRIAN

(*Laughing*) If you like peanut butter and crackers, cheddar cheese and crackers, cream cheese, chives, and crackers. Not very nourishing, but better than nothing. That's what Father said at mass last Sunday. He compared the sacred host to these sandwich crackers. It was deep. Deep. You might not have heard that sermon.

MARTIN

No problem; Rita probably taped it.

BRIAN

So, Rita is the practicing Catholic in the family?

MARTIN

All Catholics are practicing
Catholics. So yes, I'm
Catholic. Irish Catholic, in
fact. The New York Yankees
of the One True Church. Also
based in The Bronx. (*They
keep working on the bags.
Martin is determined to keep
up with Brian but does so
sloppily*)

BRIAN

I'm just curious, because I
haven't met a Catholic like
you. No offense.

MARTIN

But I've met Catholics like
you. No offense.

BRIAN

(*Laughs*) Just trying to
reconcile what you say with
what our teachers teach. I
mean last week, what was
it? "You must eat the flesh of
the God and drink the
wine... "//

MARTIN

"Truly, truly, I say to you, unless you eat the flesh of the Son of Man and drink His blood, you have no life in you." (*Pause*) The Gospel According to John.

BRIAN

Yes, that's it exactly. How did you know that if you didn't go to mass?

MARTIN

My wife takes notes.

BRIAN

What a good person!

MARTIN

(*Nodding*) And don't think she doesn't know it. The doctors call it pathological altruism.

BRIAN

You really don't go with her to mass on Sunday?

MARTIN

No. My wife and I have a
basic procedural
disagreement on the subject
of worship. At the Last
Supper, Jesus tells the
disciples: "Do this in
memory of me." But He
doesn't say how often.
Remember, this is God
talking here. God's looking
at infinity. And He
apparently has a very long
memory. From that
perspective, one mass is not
too few, a million are not too
many. So, you might say that
I'm just milking the clock.

BRIAN

That sounds like Buddhism
to me.

MARTIN

Milking the clock? I don't
think so.

BRIAN

No, the thing about one mass not being too few, a million not being too many. That's like Nichiren Shosu Buddhism. (*Dreamily*) One Daimoku is not too few, one million Daimoku is not too many. (*Sees that Martin is now the puzzled one*) *Nam myoho renge kyoho.* Chanting? Lotus sutra?

MARTIN

How do you know all this stuff? George Harrison get to you as a kid?

BRIAN

I studied Buddhism. (*Big smile*) Made the rounds of the world's great religions before finally settling upon Holy Mother Church. Nothing else ever clicked. No passion. And then... (*Gestures to the church above*) this. And you? Ever experiment with other faiths?

MARTIN

(*Seeking to keep up filling bags while they talk*) Nah, I swore off experiments after that deadly batch of LSD I cooked up in chemistry lab in high school. I've been a Catholic – and only a Catholic — since the moment I was conceived as a result of my mother's catastrophic misreading of a rhythm-method pamphlet.

BRIAN

So, you're a cradle catholic.

MARTIN

I'm a what? (*Even sloppier bag-filling*)

BRIAN

Someone who was born into the faith and therefore didn't actually have to choose his faith.

MARTIN

A cradle catholic? Catchy. Who came up with that one?

BRIAN

I don't know. It just means
that you didn't have to find
the Church; the Church
found you. Not that I'm
making a value judgment
here. (*Laughs self-
consciously*)

MARTIN

Right.

BRIAN

But, if you love the Lord our
God with all your heart,
mind, and strength,
wouldn't you want to spend
that tiny amount of time
each week at Mass?

MARTIN

Kind of a trick question
there, Brian. Only God is
Lord over the consciences of
men. Saint Augustine said
that, I think.

BRIAN

(*Aghast at the way MARTIN
is filling the bags*) That's
wrong. Completely wrong.
(*MARTIN* looks confused.)

MARTIN

I'm pretty sure it was Saint
Augustine.

BRIAN

Not that, the way you're
filling the bags. (*Points to
the poster*)

MARTIN

(*Looks at the poster, then
back at the bags then back at
the poster, back at the bags*)
Hey, I'm doing my best here.

BRIAN

(*Keeps pointing to poster*)
Sister Catherine wants the
moisturizing conditioner to
go with the moisturizing
shampoo and the oily hair
conditioner to go with the
oily hair shampoo. (*MARTIN
looks at BRIAN with a
mixture of pity and
amusement*) Those are the
rules.

MARTIN

These are for the homeless,
right? (*BRIAN nods*) Living
under bridges, sleeping in
rat-infested squats?

BRIAN

I know, I know. Sister is
pretty strict.

MARTIN

So, just to recap: Someone
living in a cardboard box,
begging twelve hours a day
with the most horrible
people in the history of the
world stepping over him.
Worse: pretending that he's
not even there. Suffers from
bug bites, rashes, open head
wounds. Dirt caked from his
ankles to his eyes,
hallucinates that he's still in
the mosh pit at an April 23,
1971 Grateful Dead concert.
With New Riders of the
Purple Sage as the opening
act. No, Poco. And this
dainty little sack is
bestowed upon him, he
takes it, and examines it
carefully and then he says:
"Excuse me; point of order,
Your Worship. I think you've
given me the wrong
conditioner. I'm the guy
with the terribly dry hair."

BRIAN

We don't just *give* it to them.
Sister Catherine Imelda
insists that we let them
choose.

MARTIN

Sister Catherine Imelda?
(*Pondering the name*)

BRIAN

She says that humans have
free will. We need to
empower them by letting
them know that they have
all sorts of choices.

MARTIN

Conditioner is empowering?
(*Strokes his hair*) If only I'd
known sooner.

BRIAN

Sister Catherine does this
with everything. All of us are
free to make good or bad
choices.

MARTIN

Sister Catherine Imelda says
that?

BRIAN

All the time. And then right
after it she says, "But there
was only one perfect man,
and they crucified him."

MARTIN

(*Stunned*) Only one perfect
man and they crucified him.
Good material. Old school.
What does she look like?

BRIAN

Sister? Very old: Late
seventies, but sharp.

MARTIN

So, like fifteen years older
than me? Completely
Paleolithic?

BRIAN

(*Nodding and continuing*)
No, I didn't mean it that way.
I meant, well, she's still
really active for someone…
who's not so young
anymore. But she's strong. If
I don't stop Sister, she'd load
the car all by herself.

MARTIN

Strong? Death ray stare?
Like the sadistic prison
guard in a 1930s black-and-
white movie?

BRIAN

No! (*Horrified*) Sister is a
saint. She's just serious, very
intense. Super-focused, like
Mother Teresa even.

MARTIN

"From silly devotions, and
sour-faced saints, good Lord,
deliver us." (*BRIAN looks
puzzled and more than a
little concerned.*) That's from
a real saint. Saint Teresa of
Avila.

BRIAN

You certainly know your
stuff: the indulgences, the
saints. Impressive.

MARTIN

Not bad for a cradle catholic,
right? Catholic college. Back
when you still had to take
Theology, not the *I Ching*.

BRIAN

I love the saints. Love them.
Which saint were you
named after? (*Now it's
MARTIN who looks confused*)
Saint Martin of Tours?
Martin De Poor-hez?

MARTIN

(*Pronouncing correctly*) It's
De Porres. Then, of course,
there was Saint Martin, the
patron saint of not shutting
the fuck up.

BRIAN

Whoa! They have a saint for
that?

MARTIN

Saint Martin. Elected Pope in
649. Persecuted.
Imprisoned. Tortured.
Couldn't stop running at the
mouth. Ticked people off.
Martyred in 655 AD. Cradle
catholic.

BRIAN

I was a little disappointed
that there's no Saint Brian.
Well, not exactly. There is
one: Bryan of Arrowsmith,

MARTIN

Aerosmith? Dude like a
lady?

BRIAN

*Arrow*smith. And it was
Bryan with a "Y."

MARTIN

Leaves a nice opening for
you to be that first Saint
Brian. With an "I."

BRIAN

(*Embarrassed*) No, thanks.
For the record, that Bryan
was hanged, drawn and
quartered for the faith.

MARTIN

And your mother knew all
this? When she named you
Brian? Must have been one
tough pregnancy.

BRIAN

Oh, no! She named me after
some character named Brian
in a movie she saw. She
wasn't religious. More of a
film club person. (*Shrugs*)
Died young. But when I

started to think about converting, I wanted to find some sort of saintly connection. I mean... (*Quite enthusiastic*) Saints!!! Sister chose her saint when she went into the convent: Catherine of Alexandria. Martyr.

MARTIN

Natch.

BRIAN

And Imelda was a medieval Italian saint who one day gets this incredible vision of the host coming to her, and then she dies in this spectacular ecstasy of pure spiritual love and passion. (Sees that Martin is still just shoving the little bottles helter-skelter into the baggies.) Oh, you have to fix those. Sister isn't going to let us take them that way.

MARTIN

I'm kind of immersed in my own spectacularly intense baggie-filling ecstasy right now. "The conditioner you shall always have with you."

Door behind MARTIN opens: SISTER enters; she looks at Brian, then Martin and goes over to examine his pile of bags.

SISTER CATHERINE IMELDA

This is wrong. All wrong. (*Holds up a baggie and spills its contents in front of Martin and then holds up another one for inspection*) Wrong. (*Again, she spills its contents before picking up another one to examine*) This one is right. (Now looking intently at Martin) One for three might get you a spot on the Yankees, but it doesn't get the job done here.

MARTIN

(*Picks up his other bags and puts them into a box on the table*) Actually, (*Staring at her*) I'm a Mets fan.

SISTER
CATHERINE
IMELDA

(*Winces*) Well, we can't
make errors around here at
the rate the New York Mets
do. (*Gestures toward the
poster with the instructions*)
Follow the rules.

BRIAN

Sister, that's my fault. This
is his first time. He brought
this huge stash of little
bottles his wife collects. And
then he volunteered to help.

SISTER
CATHERINE
IMELDA

Everyone always means well
when they come here. But
the road to Hell is paved
with good intentions, We
leave in under an hour. Let's
pick up the pace.

*She and MARTIN both look each
other over very carefully. SISTER
exits with a box through the door
to the outside*

MARTIN

Jesus, it's her.

BRIAN

Who?

MARTIN

My eighth-grade
schoolteacher.

BRIAN

No! Are you sure? She
recognized you?

MARTIN

We had a moment.

BRIAN

This is amazing.

MARTIN

Well, I'm certainly amazed,
Brian-o.

BRIAN

You should be! It's a kind of
grace. You wander in and
decide to stay to do good
works and then you're
reunited with your old
teacher. It's like a personal
miracle. (He moves a
completed box over to exit
area where other boxes are
stacked)

MARTIN

Yeah, a miracle, like when a
Nazi hunter just happens to
run into an SS
*einsatzgruppen
oberkommandant* while
walking down the street in
Buenos Aires. (*BRIAN recoils
at this comment. MARTIN
stuffs the toiletries back into
the baggies with even less
precision*) I almost didn't
recognize her without the
(*Gestures*) wimple and the
habit and the cape. It's like
seeing Eichmann out of
uniform. But those eyes, that
voice. I'd know them
anywhere. It's her.

BRIAN

You and Sister didn't get
along?

MARTIN

People like me didn't get
along with nuns. But back
then, the church was
different — at least for us
cradle Catholics.

BRIAN

I didn't mean to offend you
with that term. It's just
something they say in class
to distinguish between those
of us who are converting
and those ...//

MARTIN

Who take our faith for
granted? That's okay. The
people teaching you... I
know the type...//

BRIAN

The number of things we
have to learn is phenomenal.

MARTIN

And how are you doing? Top
of the class, I bet?

BRIAN

I think I'm ready for the next
step.

MARTIN

What are they teaching you?

BRIAN

The catechesis — the
teachings. I'm past the
catechumen's stage, did my
rite of election. Almost done
with the scrutinies. And
then... God willing...

MARTIN

(*Ignoring him*) What did
they give you to study?
Baltimore Catechism? The
Acts of the Apostles? *The
One True Faith for Dummies*?

BRIAN

(*Taking a slightly superior
tone*) I'm pretty sure the
Baltimore Catechism is out
of date. We get books, PDFs,
so we can read the material
online. All about the Trinity,
the sacraments, Church law.

MARTIN

Seven deadly sins? Seven
dwarfs? Seven sacraments?
Come on: out with them.

BRIAN

(*Starts to recite*) Baptism, Confirmation, Eucharist, Penance, Anointing of the Sick. Matrimony...//

MARTIN

(*Interrupting*) Anointing of the Sick? Anointing of the Sick? They're not sick; they're dying. What kind of New Age bunkum is that? Are you talking about Extreme Unction? Well, don't water it down. It's *Extreme* Unction, not Intermediary Unction. Real Catholicism, Brian, is an extreme sport and real Catholics call it Extreme Unction. We are the X games of religion: original sin, celibacy, hair shirts, drinking of blood, martyrs. No other religion is even close to us when it comes to martyrs. Gory to God in the highest.

BRIAN

Isn't that supposed to be
glory to God? (*Catching on*)
Oh, right. Well, since you
ask, our classes are all about
the profession of faith,
celebration of the Christian
mystery, living our lives in
Christ, prayer. And the rules
of the Church: Those are
super-important.

MARTIN

Rules? That's not faith.
That's membership. Faith is
believing when you have no
reason to believe.

BRIAN

That doesn't make sense.
(*Doubting himself*) Does it?
(*Resumes packing*)

MARTIN

Who said being Catholic
should make sense?
(*Stuffing the bags so that
they form a precarious pile*

on the table) I'm just saying
that being Catholic — really
Catholic — it's not for the
queasy, me bucko. Real
Catholics can stomach St.
Matthew being blinded by
drills into his eyes, Isaac
Jogues getting his fingers
gnawed off by the Iroquois,
and Saint Barnabas being
stoned and burned and
dismembered — although
not necessarily in that order
— with bones and entrails
strewn about everywhere.

BRIAN

This is pretty different from
the Catholicism I've been
learning. Our focus is more...
cerebral....//

MARTIN

By the way, a professional,
well-handled stoning
provides an excellent source
of collectible souvenir relics.
Case in point: St.
Bartholomew. Flayed alive
by the Armenians?
Armenians, what can I tell
you? Things always get out

of hand with those guys. No, real Catholics don't flinch looking at those paintings of him, in the Sistine Chapel, holding strands of his own skin before the heathens behead him. (*Beat*) Patron saint of tanners, by the way.

The door to the outside opens again and SISTER CATHERINE IMELDA returns. She looks more carefully at MARTIN this time.

> SISTER
> CATHERINE
> IMELDA

There seems to be more talk than work going on in here.

> MARTIN

Brian and I were discussing Church history, Sister.

BRIAN busily grabs filled boxes to stack at exit.

> SISTER
> CATHERINE
> IMELDA

Am I supposed to know you?

> MARTIN

Do you know me, Sister?
Sister CATHERINE IMELDA

(*Shrugs*) St. Anthony's. Richardson Avenue.

MARTIN

Right borough, wrong corner. St. Jerome's. Graduated. 1965.

SISTER CATHERINE IMELDA

Doesn't ring a bell.

MARTIN

Give it time, Sister.

She looks at him for a long moment and then exits again, taking a box outside.

BRIAN

That's too bad. I was really hoping that Sister would remember you.

MARTIN

It'll come to her. Trust me.

BRIAN

There weren't a lot of active Catholics where I grew up. There wasn't much religion at all outside of the temple —

SISTER returns, striding briskly to where MARTIN is leaning up against the table and puts her nose right into his face.

> SISTER
> CATHERINE
> IMELDA

Altar boy.

> MARTIN

(*Folds his hands in prayer and then genuflects*) *Introibo ad altare Dei*: I go to the altar of God. *Ad Deum qui laetificat juventutem meam*: To God, the joy of my youth. (*Smiles*) Got a dime for an old Altar boy, Sister?

> BRIAN

How did you learn to speak Latin like that?

> MARTIN

Cradle catholic thing, kiddo. (*Extends his hand to Sister*) My feelings were getting hurt wondering if you were going to remember me,

Sister. (*She takes his hand
and shakes it warily*)

SISTER
CATHERINE
IMELDA

I am seventy-seven ears old.
Seventy-seven. I'm lucky to
remember my own name.
(*Looks at MARTIN again*)
1965. St. Jerome's.
Alexander Avenue. The
Bronx. The Mass was still in
Latin?

MARTIN

It changed after you kicked
me off the altar boys.
Though the events were
probably not directly
related.

*SISTER does not react, but moves
to the stack of boxes. BRIAN is
confused by what was said.*

BRIAN

Must feel quite special to
meet someone you taught
over fifty years ago.

                    SISTER
                    CATHERINE
                    IMELDA

Special? (*Eyes MARTIN*) Oh,
there were so many
students. Too many. Besides,
I didn't stick with the
teaching. *(She starts to pick
up a box)*

                    MARTIN

No memory at all? Just my
pride making me think I had
some special quality, I guess.

                    SISTER
                    CATHERINE
                    IMELDA

Pride goeth before a fall.

                    BRIAN

I know that one. Old
Testament. Right?

                    MARTIN

"Pride goeth before
destruction, and a haughty
spirit before a fall." Proverbs
16:18. To be absolutely
precise.

BRIAN

For a Catholic, you sure can
nail those Old Testament
quotes. (*Seeks to explain*)
One of our teachers said that
quoting Scripture is usually
kind of a fundamentalist
thing.

MARTIN

(*Ignoring BRIAN and
following SISTER, while
resuming stuffing bags*) Did
he? Well, now. Just for the
record, Brian, pride is one of
the seven deadly sins.
Learned that in Sister's
class. "Lucifer Glares,
Grandma Slowly Writes
Endless Prayers" Lust,
Gluttony, Greed, Sloth,
Wrath, Envy, Pride. (*To
BRIAN*) And pride includes
presumption, hypocrisy,
hardheartedness. See what a
good teacher Sister was?

BRIAN

I do.

SISTER
CATHERINE
IMELDA

If you're the proof of my superb teaching, God forgive me. Do you still live in the parish?

MARTIN

(*Shaking head*) Eventually, my mother got us out of The Bronx. You remember my mother: Maeve Mahoney? (*SISTER shakes her head*) I graduated college — English major. Managed to miss out on both Vietnam and Woodstock. Stayed out of jail, too.

SISTER
CATHERINE
IMELDA

That says more about the goodness of your mother. And father. (*MARTIN stares harder at her*) And now?

MARTIN

I'm an involuntarily retired sportswriter with three grown children who generally seem to tolerate me. None of them ever missed a meal. All of them graduated from college, (*SISTER indicates she seeks more information*) And I've been married for almost forty years. (*Emphatically*) Without the help of any marriage counseling. Professional or otherwise.

SISTER CATHERINE IMELDA

That says more about the goodness of your wife. So, are you a good man? (*Taps her chest hard*) In here?

MARTIN

Now there's a trick question if there ever was one. No one is good but God alone, right, Sister? (*To BRIAN*) Mark, 10:18. (*To SISTER again*) There was only one perfect man, Sister. And look what happened to Him.

BRIAN

You are like a walking *Google Books Bible*. (*To SISTER*) Martin is amazing, isn't he, Sister? We should get him to help teach the Rite of Christian Initiation classes. (*Keeps filling baggies, automatically*)

SISTER
CATHERINE
IMELDA

(*Ignoring BRIAN and regarding MARTIN carefully*) No, no, no. Those bags are all wrong. (*MARTIN sweeps them into one of the empty cardboard boxes*)

MARTIN

"Kill them all, Let God sort them out!" The conditioner, I mean.

SISTER
CATHERINE
IMELDA

Oh, I see, Mr. Clever Quotes is in the room! Well, if you're going to be spouting sayings from some obscure 12th century French monk , at least get it right. "Kill them all. God will recognize his own."

MARTIN

That's not the way the Hell's Angels print it on their t-shirts. And it's thirteenth century.

BRIAN

(*Perplexed*) I can fix them, Sister. (*Makes a move to do so, but SISTER slightly flustered, puts up her hand to stop him*)

SISTER
CATHERINE
IMELDA

We have enough of those anyway. Let's do some more of the crackers. (*Starts to kick a box to the side, but BRIAN hustles it off to the car*) So, you came to give alms to the poor? (*BRIAN reenters immediately and then repeats his quick exit*)

MARTIN

No, just to drop off toiletries. But Brian looked like he needed a little help. And miracle of miracles, we are reunited. Amazing grace, isn't it, Sister? Like Matthew 18:12–14 — the Lost Sheep?

SISTER
CATHERINE
IMELDA

Why not the Prodigal Son? Luke 15:11–32

MARTIN

Or Saint Paul: "The day of the Lord will come like a thief in the night." (*Claps his hands*) Sudden destruction.

BRIAN

(*Returning again*) This is like a Roman Catholic quiz show! How do you two have all this scripture memorized?

MARTIN

Catholic indoctrination from kindergarten all the way through college — even summer school. Then so many seasons on the road covering losing teams in dreary hotel rooms with nothing but a Bible to distract me. Well, that and Fox News. A head for obscure stats didn't hurt.

SISTER
CATHERINE
IMELDA

Were you always (Gestures, searching for words) this way?

MARTIN

Forced retirement added the finishing touches to the masterpiece. But you're still about the Lord's business, right?

BRIAN

(*Returning to the tables with
the new supplies of crackers,
carrots, etc.*) It's a blessing to
have you, Martin. (*Both
MARTIN and SISTER give
him a long look*)

SISTER
CATHERINE
IMELDA

(*Pointing to BRIAN*) He's a
millionaire, this one. An
honest-to-goodness
millionaire.

BRIAN

I don't think Martin cares
about that. (*Goes downstage
briefly to bring more water
bottles to the tables*)

SISTER
CATHERINE
IMELDA

And he comes down here to
help me. Volunteers out of
the goodness of his own
heart. Not because his wife
sent him.

MARTIN

You said he was *a*
millionaire. Just one?

BRIAN

(*Embarrassed*) I've been
Super-Blessed.

MARTIN

Oh. A multi-millionaire?

SISTER
CATHERINE
IMELDA

Is that any of your business?

MARTIN

Just making conversation to
help us pass the time. Or we
could sing instead.
Remember this golden oldie,
Sister? (*Begins to sing in a
rousing voice. BRIAN quite
enjoys this surprising display,
but SISTER becomes
increasingly agitated by the
singing*) Tantum ergo
Sacramentum Veneremur
cernui: Et antiquum
documentum Novo cedat
ritui: Praestet fides
supplementum Sensuum
defectui. (*Gathers his breath
to continue*)

53

SISTER
CATHERINE
IMELDA

For the love of God… It's sacrilege to sing that as a joke.

MARTIN

Sacrilege! That's what you said when I sang it that way in eighth grade. Remember? You threw me out of religion class. But I went to the library and found a book explaining exactly how Saint Thomas Aquinas, who wrote it, wanted it sung out. And when I informed the whole class, you were so happy. Ecstatic. Coming back now? (*No reaction*) Being here with you and Brian is bringing back that old-time religion for me. *Laus et jubilatio. Adeste fidelis. Dies irae.* (to an increasingly baffled Brian, while moving some crackers and carrots to his table so that he can bag them) So, Brian, what did you do to earn your millions?

BRIAN

I created a predictive
algorithm for a shopping
network. (He is back at his
table)

MARTIN

A predictive algorithm! Was
it a mystical algorithm?

BRIAN

(*Dismissive*) There's no such
thing. Algorithms are just
sets of rules that do their
logical operations the way
you write them. There's
nothing mystical about it.

MARTIN

But lucrative.

BRIAN

(*Reluctantly*) Yes, for which I
now thank God, because in a
way it led me here. Sister
says: God writes straight...
(*Waiting with a smile for her
to finish it*)

SISTER
CATHERINE
IMELDA

... in crooked lines.

BRIAN

But that's all behind me
now.

MARTIN

Why? You could be the
patron saint of predictive
algorithms. (*SISTER snorts
derisively and crosses over to
stack of boxes*) So, how many
millions?

SISTER
CATHERINE
IMELDA

Stop badgering him.

MARTIN

(*To BRIAN*) Oh, come on,
how many? Sorry, being a
journalist for so many years,
I simply can't stop asking
questions.

SISTER
CATHERINE
IMELDA

Journalist? Journalist?
(*Carrying two boxes, she
starts to leave shooing
BRIAN away as he attempts
to take them away from her*)
You weren't a journalist; you
were a sportswriter. (Exits.)

BRIAN

Hey, Martin, go easy on
Sister, please?

MARTIN

Sure. (*Pause in bagging*)
Moving right along then,
how many millions?

BRIAN

Look, Martin...

MARTIN

Fess up. Come on.

BRIAN

Okay. Okay. (*Pause, then in a
low* voice) Fifty. (*MARTIN
whistles and reacts wildly*)
But it's not important
because I'm giving it all
away.

MARTIN

Fifty? (*Draws in the air*) Fifty
million? And you're giving it
all away? Not to her, I hope?

BRIAN

Sister? No. I mean she
suggested some of the
charities, but it's basically
going to the poor.

MARTIN

(*Silence and then softly*)
Alms to the poor.

BRIAN

(*Enthusiastic*) That's what
Sister called it. Alms to the
poor. (*Smiling, as if waiting
for another expected
question*) Don't you want to
know why?

MARTIN

(*Shakes his head*) Maybe
later. (*He contemplates the
items to be inserted into the
snack bags. Then, while
BRIAN has his head down
bagging, he pitches one of
the food packets at him, who
eliciting a shocked reaction*)

MARTIN

Fifty million! Now turn the
other cheek so I can get a
shot at that one. (*Aims while
BRIAN defends himself*)

BRIAN

Hey, Sister is going to come
in here.

MARTIN

Sister! She's out there laughing hysterically. Juggling little bottles of goo in here in the middle of the night because I felt sorry for you. And then it turns out that you're worth fifty million bucks. Trust me, St. Brian of Briarcliff, the meter is running. You're getting a bill for my services in the morning (*Looking more directly at Brian, who is smiling widely*) Just for the record, are you enjoying this?

BRIAN

(*Resuming bagging*) In a way. To have someone working alongside you makes everything go faster. And for all your joking around, I get you. Only a good person would stay to help at this hour.

MARTIN

You *get* me? (*Sorting his items into piles but distractedly*) I think consorting with your fellow algorithmaniacs all day long has warped your mind. You sound like my mom, another cheerfully delusional introvert.

BRIAN

This is not about reality. It's about charity, Mister Cradle Catholic. And you should know that. (*Intoning while pausing work*) "So faith, hope, charity abide, these three. But the greatest of these is charity."

MARTIN

(*Resuming his bagging, but hesitantly*) Personal question: Have you been scanned for a brain tumor? Any history of premature dementia in your family? Honest, Brian, I think you need to get this thing checked out.

BRIAN

(*Patiently but still amusedly*)
That last quote was from St.
Paul. See, I knew one! I even
put it on my Facebook page.
(*Reciting but eagerly*)
"Charity is patient and kind,
(*MARTIN pitches another
packet but BRIAN catches
this one*) charity is not
jealous or boastful; it is not
arrogant or rude. (*Another
packet thrown, and BRIAN
recites more quickly*) Charity
does not insist on its own
way; it is not irritable or
resentful; (*MARTIN pitches
another packet; again, a nice
catch*) it does not rejoice at
wrong but rejoices in the
right. Charity bears all
things, (*MARTIN makes as if
to pitch another packet but
stops; BRIAN finishes
strongly*) Believes all things,
hopes all things, endures all
things."

MARTIN

You forgot the part about "Charity vaunteth not itself, is not puffed up." I think that was Ben and Jerry's original motto. (*Looking confusedly at his piles and bags*) No, Tom's of Maine. Anyway, what are we actually doing here?

BRIAN

(*Smiling, he indicates another instructional illustration poster*) More of those different rules you like so much. (*Smiles*) Yes, coders do sarcasm. (*Demonstrating*) Packages of crackers, small bags of baby carrots, and small bottles of water. And Sister's rules on organization. (*MARTIN regards a package of peanut butter crackers and then starts to open it. BRIAN looks at him in alarm*)

MARTIN

Sister's rules. Organization.
(*With a cracker in his mouth,
he begins to assemble these
packets throughout BRIAN's
instructions with even less
caution than the previous
batch*)

BRIAN

(*Frowning at what MARTIN
is doing*) It's pretty simple.
Peanut butter crackers, a
bag of baby carrots, one
bottle of water in one
baggie. Cheese and crackers.
The same thing. And if you
come across these little
packages of salami? Just put
them in a baggie with a
bottle of water and carrots.

MARTIN

What's so special about the
carrots? (*Takes a bite and
then spits it across the floor*)
I bet these are a big hit.
(*Assembling these bags just
as quickly and haphazardly
as the previous batches*)

BRIAN

We try to promote healthy
eating. (*Summoning his
nerve*) Those are only
supposed to be for…

MARTIN

(*Continuing to open the
package*) Poor people?

BRIAN

Our recipients.

MARTIN

Our recipients? Nice touch. I
guess Starbucks was already
using "Guests." (*Eats one of
the crackers*) Piquant.

BRIAN

But now there's less to share
with the poor.

MARTIN

Don't worry. (*Takes out his
wallet and extracts some
singles*) For each one of
these packets I eat I'm going
to put a dollar bill in a bag.
In fact, I'm going to put a
dollar bill in a bag for every
packet you eat as well. Hey!

Why don't you stick a dollar
bill inside fifty million
individual baggies, Brian?
With a little bottle of
conditioner. For dry hair.

BRIAN

We don't give them money.

MARTIN

Them? You mean our
recipients?

BRIAN

Sister says it's not a good
idea.

MARTIN

(*Opening another package
and putting another dollar
into one of the food bags*)
Then this will be our little
secret. 49,999,999 to go.

BRIAN

When you hear the words
"fifty million dollars," it's a
shock. I understand that.
That's a lot of money for an
algorithm.

MARTIN

Predictive algorithm, Brian.

BRIAN

Whatever. (*Resumes bagging*) Then the company got bought and it went public and all of a sudden, my stock was worth fifty million bucks.

MARTIN

Oh, like a gigantic sack of cash dropped out of the sky and landed on your head. Stop with the false modesty. You invented something worth fifty million dollars. Don't you think that makes you a very unusual person?

BRIAN

For today. But tomorrow someone will come along and create a better algorithm. (*Sees that MARTIN is puzzled and pauses bagging*) See all this stuff: bottles, crackers, toothbrushes. To an algorithm, it's data. All a predictive algorithm does is spit out what the people associated with this mishmash of barcodes might purchase. Algorithms are

just gossips. Tattle-tales.
Snitches. Dumpster-diving
reporters. (*Puts his hands up
defensively*)

MARTIN

Now we're getting personal.

BRIAN

My algorithm just analyzes
"clicks" and "likes." Then it
predicts what everyone will
want to see, even if they
would swear to you they
don't want to see it. The
algorithm calculates exactly
when there'll be a warming
of the skin, a micro-smile, a
little more blood rushing to
the brain, when they think
they're happy. It's not
important. It's a tool. That's
all.

MARTIN

Yeah, but a tool that... //

BRIAN

It's code; it's not a cure for
cancer. And it won't save
anybody's soul. And the

money is just fifty million things getting in the way of what I really desire. It's a distraction.

MARTIN

A distraction? Is that understatement or irony?

BRIAN

Coders don't do irony and we don't do understatement. But we are good at getting things done. (*Holds up a baggie*) The bags? Okay?

MARTIN

All right. (*Back to work mode, but agitated*) She really has you…

BRIAN

(*Reacting to MARTIN's look of disbelief*) I know that all this seems silly, but it's the way Sister organizes things. She's a super-good guide for me. In fact, I hope to take the vows as soon as I can. When she says that I'm ready.

MARTIN

You need a guide to take your baptismal vows?

BRIAN

The Baptismal vows are just
the beginning. I have a
calling to become... //

MARTIN

I can baptize you right here
and now. We have water.
(*Opens one of the water
bottles and holds it in one
hand*) So, we're good to go.
(*MARTIN places his hand on
BRIAN's shoulder, which
stops him from moving
away*) This whole operation
will only take about thirty
seconds. (*Goes into his
Baltimore Catechism voice*)
"Who can administer
baptism? The priest is the
usual minister of baptism,
but, if there is danger that
someone will die without
baptism, anyone else may
and should baptize." You *are*
driving to The Bronx
tonight, right? Talk about
risking your life for Christ!
Therefore, (Sprinkles water
on BRIAN, who dances back)
"I baptize thee in the name
of the Father, and of the Son,
and of the Holy Ghost."

BRIAN

(*Behind them, quietly,
SISTER has reentered the
room in response to the
commotion and observes
them*) Hey, I don't have a
change of clothes.

SISTER
CATHERINE
IMELDA

So now Mr. Furloughed
Sportswriter is John the
Baptist. (*They whirl around
and see her*) Well, he doesn't
need your help. Brian
already has Baptism of
Desire: When someone loves
God above all things and
desires to do all that is
necessary for salvation. (*To
MARTIN, while pointing at
BRIAN*) Anyone determined
to take the other vows has
that desire.

MARTIN

What other vows?

BRIAN

Obedience, chastity, and
poverty.

MARTIN

Poverty, chastity, and
obedience. Get them in the
right order.

SISTER
CATHERINE
IMELDA

He's joining the monastery.
Becoming a monk.

MARTIN

No way.

BRIAN

The Brothers of Mercy. A
partly cloistered order. If
they'll have me. But I have to
wait a year after being
baptized.

SISTER
CATHERINE
IMELDA

At least a year.

MARTIN

Jesus. You kept on spinning
the religious roulette wheel
until you hit "Give away all
your money and become a
semi-cloistered monk"?

BRIAN

Sometimes I feel like I'm dreaming all of this.

MARTIN

This is unlike any dream I ever had. And I used to smoke Lebanese Hash. (*To SISTER*) That was long after our relationship ended, Sister.

SISTER
CATHERINE
IMELDA

We never had a relationship.

BRIAN

You do have a wicked sense of humor, Martin.

SISTER
CATHERINE
IMELDA

Wicked.

MARTIN

Why become a monk? Because you're flat broke after giving away fifty million dollars?

SISTER
CATHERINE
IMELDA

(*To MARTIN*) Who
appointed you Devil's
Advocate? Look to the care
of your own soul. Remind
me again: Why are you
here?

MARTIN

To do what my wife tells me
to do. Just to keep peace in
the valley. But running into
you today has been like
smacking a mystical four-
bagger. Sorry my mother
couldn't be here. She's in
Heaven awaiting the
resurrection.

SISTER
CATHERINE
IMELDA

Don't you ever stop in the
middle of this spiel of yours
and say, 'What the hell am I
doing here?' (*BRIAN gasps
at her use of the word "hell"*)

MARTIN

Sister, I'm sixty-four years old. I'm constantly asking myself what I'm doing here. "What the Fuck am I doing here?" is my personal mantra.

BRIAN

Martin, language! (Martin mischievously covers his mouth with his hand.) She means: What are you doing with your life? (*To SISTER*) Right, Sister?

SISTER
CATHERINE
IMELDA

(*Addressing MARTIN to get an answer*) Since you feel so free to strut in here and ask questions of everyone else

*MARTIN is silent and looks back
and forth between the two of
them. BRIAN, with palms
gesticulating, urges some sort of
response. SISTER stares and then
she pounds the table. MARTIN
jumps a little and then speaks.*

MARTIN

To know, love, and serve
God? (*SISTER turns away
disgustedly*) I just do
whatever is right in front of
me to keep things moving.
And tonight's schedule is a
surprise reunion with my
most memorable teacher,
while doing the baggie
shuffle. To be is to do. To do
is to be. Do be do be doo. I
got that off the wall of a bar
in The Bronx and it became
my philosophy at a very
early age. Again, after our
relationship ended, Sister.

SISTER
CATHERINE
IMELDA

I don't remember any
relationship. I don't
remember you, period.

MARTIN

Now that would have hurt
my mother, your forgetting
our connection. You always
took a special interest in her.

SISTER
CATHERINE
IMELDA

I don't live in the past. I
concentrate on the time God
has left me. Now. We leave
in twenty minutes. Box up
what isn't in bags and we'll
give it out loose. (*Exits with
a box through the door to the
outside, without looking at
MARTIN*)

BRIAN

What do you have against
her? (Placing packets in a
box)

MARTIN

Nothing in particular.
Everything in general.
(*Pause*) She remembers.
(*Stuffs a bag in the most
random, cavalier manner*)
She does.

BRIAN

Grudges aren't good for us. I
learned that during my
Buddhist period.

MARTIN

According to some
prominent theologians,
holding grudges is the long-
lost eighth sacrament.

*MARTIN eats crackers and
salami, stuffing dollar bills into a
bag every time he does so.*

BRIAN

But that's not what we're
here for, is it? Settling of
accounts, revenge?

MARTIN

What are we here for, Brian?

BRIAN

(*With a smile*) To drop off a
large bag of small,
complimentary shampoos.
Organized almsgiving
(*MARTIN groans*) You came
here to help, Martin, not to
get angry and upset.

MARTIN

No, I came here to escape
Rita's bellyaching about
losing our mortgage-interest
deduction.

BRIAN

I'd love to meet her.

MARTIN

And she you. A baby monk;
they make the cutest pets.
Like marmosets. But when
they grow up...

*SISTER enters the room and
looks at MARTIN. She sees all the
cracker wrappers and empty
bottles of water and picks up the
broom to sweep them. Then she
eyes a bag with a dollar bill in it.
She holds it up.*

SISTER
CATHERINE
IMELDA

What is this?

BRIAN

I was going to fix that, Sister.

MARTIN

It's a dollar bill, Sister.
(*Bows to her*) Render unto
Caesar the things that are
Little Caesar's. Christian
charity always make me
work up an appetite.

SISTER
CATHERINE
IMELDA

One of the most important
rules of the Midnight Run is
that we don't give out
money directly.

MARTIN

How does that rule stack up
against "Love thy neighbor
as thyself?" I think Brian has
that one on his Facebook
page.

SISTER
CATHERINE
IMELDA

Did you ever hear the
saying: "All Heretics Quote
Scripture"?

MARTIN

Sister, "heretic" is a positive term of
endearment for me.

SISTER
CATHERINE
IMELDA

You still consider yourself a
real Catholic?

MARTIN

I do.

*BRIAN braces for an explosion,
but SISTER instead pulls up a
chair and sits facing MARTIN.
She takes one of the packets of
crackers, opens it, and is poised
to take her first bite*

SISTER
CATHERINE
IMELDA

Are you going to pony up a
dollar for me? Even though I
don't remember you?

MARTIN

Of course, Sister. (*He does
so*) Perhaps the memory of
our time together is
repressed.

SISTER
CATHERINE
IMELDA

Oh no, here we go: repressed memories! I hope you're not one of those walking pity parties, still smarting from some backhand you caught in fourth grade.

MARTIN

No, I got smacked around enough at home. As you know.

SISTER
CATHERINE
IMELDA

So many want "closure." Is that it? Did I catch you with the Communion wine? Or in the cloakroom with a girl?

MARTIN

Not me, Sister. At least you never caught me.

SISTER
CATHERINE
IMELDA

But I taught you. Or so you claim. (*Hesitates*) I didn't like teaching. In fact, I dreaded it. I thought teaching would be like learning. (*Shakes her head*) Two completely different things.

BRIAN

How did you deal with that dread? (*Continuing to work*)

SISTER
CATHERINE
IMELDA

I offered it up for the souls in Purgatory. Thy will be done. Eventually, after a few painful years in the classroom, Mother Superior suggested an assignment more suited to my talents.

MARTIN

Border patrol? Swiss Guard?

SISTER
CATHERINE
IMELDA

Helping the poor. Plain and
simple. A lot more
rewarding than trying to
knock sense into the likes of
you.

BRIAN

You never told me about
this, Sister.

SISTER
CATHERINE
IMELDA

(*Rising*) You're not father
confessor yet, Brian.

MARTIN

How could you possibly
have any sins to confess,
Sister? In your utterly
blameless and impossibly
pious life?

SISTER
CATHERINE
IMELDA

Everyone needs confession
and reconciliation. Just one
more thing you have wrong.

BRIAN

But seriously, Sister, what
sins could you possibly
commit?

SISTER
CATHERINE
IMELDA

Anything any other human
could. Nuns are human. A
vocation is not a shield. To
be human is to be someone
with feelings. Sometimes
those feelings take us in the
wrong direction. And when
they do, we fall from grace.
We sin.

MARTIN

I think it was Kierkegaard
who said that sin...//

SISTER
CATHERINE
IMELDA

Spare us the quotes, Mr.
Used-To-Be-A-Sportswriter
(*Turning to BRIAN*) Thinking
the religious are pure is a
common misconception,
Brian. (*She takes another
package of crackers and
motions to MARTIN to pay
up*)

MARTIN

Common. (*He ponies up the dollar*)

SISTER
CATHERINE
IMELDA

(*Unwrapping the packet, the whole time still talking to BRIAN*) Even nuns have to get used to being nuns. Moving towards a vocation is a long path. No one can take it in all at once. I certainly didn't. Not at seventeen, with my father smirking, not believing it was going to last. And my mother wailing in the background. Like it was my wake.

BRIAN

That's kind of sad.

SISTER
CATHERINE
IMELDA

She knew I would never be the same to her, that I was gone. But the changes in our new lives don't happen all at once. There are stages,

85

Brian, and each stage separates you a little more from the world. It was strange to still be human like everyone else but somehow also different, apart. Not just leaving my parents, but my brothers, friends, everyone — living in a world they would never know. This life is not for everyone.

BRIAN

But you had this wonderful new community, like anew family.

SISTER
CATHERINE
IMELDA

A different kind of family.

MARTIN

More like a team whose glory years are long in the past.

BRIAN

But the convent allows all this quiet and contemplation.

SISTER
CATHERINE
IMELDA

A little too much quiet now.
These days, we're all
doddering or dead.

BRIAN

Not you, Sister.

SISTER
CATHERINE
IMELDA

(*Ignoring him*) Everything
changed. We had no idea.
When you leave the world,
you don't expect it to come
boomeranging back into the
convent. We missed what
was going on until it crashed
in on us. The younger ones
left: married priests, ex-
priests — some of my
closest friends. One of them
married a Jewish
psychiatrist. Imagine.

MARTIN

Oy.

SISTER
CATHERINE
IMELDA

(*Stifling a chortle*) She lost
touch with me. Most did. As
they should; who wants to

spend all their time looking back at the past? A dying breed, the religious. They should put us on one of those endangered-species lists with the snow leopards and the white rhinos.

MARTIN starts to speak, but stops himself

BRIAN

But it could come back, all of it: the family, the Church, maybe lay brothers and sisters?

SISTER looks askance at him and takes another cracker out of the packet. MARTIN and BRIAN resume bagging, but at a more moderate pace than previously

MARTIN

Sister, did you know that my mother Maeve was a lay sister at the end? At a convent right near here. She kept calling herself a "lay associate," and I would ask her when she was going to make partner. But the job was scut work: cook and laundress. She did it for free.

BRIAN

Your mother sounds like she
was a *super* Catholic!

MARTIN

(*Stopping bagging*) Super.
Hall of Fame. A Nobel prize-
winning Catholic. Mom was
devoted to devotion.
Veneration of the Eucharist,
Benediction, barefoot
genuflecting pilgrimages.
And let's not forget her daily
prayers to Saint Jude, patron
saint of hopeless causes.

SISTER
CATHERINE
IMELDA

With you as a son...

MARTIN

So, you *do* remember us,
Sister?

SISTER
CATHERINE
IMELDA

One can imagine you. Your
type.

MARTIN

But not Maeve? Good
looking colleen. Red hair.
Wore too much makeup at

times, but she had her
reasons.

                BRIAN

Your mom sounds amazing.

                MARTIN

She was. Amazing. If a tad
deranged.

                SISTER
                CATHERINE
                IMELDA

She was beyond your
understanding.

                MARTIN

I thought you didn't
remember Mom, Sister.
(*SISTER bites into the
cracker*) Well, she never
forgot you. You were burned
into her memory.

                BRIAN

You got a lot of being
Catholic from your mother,
didn't you?

                MARTIN

Just the old churches' part.
The silence, the mystery.
The smell of incense. The
quiet connection to God, I
guess. And midnight mass —
singing those carols at full

volume while she held my
hand. (Pause) She couldn't
walk past a church, a bakery,
or a cemetery without
making a visit. I'm the same.

> SISTER
> CATHERINE
> IMELDA

That's not Catholicism.
That's nostalgia.

> MARTIN

It's still a kind of faith, isn't
it?

> SISTER
> CATHERINE
> IMELDA

Faith in what, exactly?

> MARTIN

The past.

> SISTER
> CATHERINE
> IMELDA

Sports (*Beat*) Writers.
(*Shaking her head*) A
peerless oxymoron. Give me
a bottle of water. All this
gabbing has me parched.
And cough up another
dollar. (*MARTIN extends the
bottle and places another
dollar in the pile*)

BRIAN

Sister, you said we shouldn't
give money. But now…

SISTER
CATHERINE
IMELDA

The only one who's infallible
is the Pope, Brian. And
things like this… It's a
discipline, not a dogma.

MARTIN

You'll find there's a lot of
that shillyshallying these
days in Holy Mother Church,
Brian.

BRIAN

If you feel this way, why call
yourself Catholic?

MARTIN

"Once an RC, always an RC,"
as the upper-class WASPs
whisper when they think we
can't hear. (*SISTER snorts*)
The show's been running for
two thousand years. Just
because the clergy
bamboozled and bullied the
faithful, covered up crimes,
buried what Christ was all
about, doesn't change my
being Catholic.

SISTER
CATHERINE
IMELDA

You can call yourself a bird,
but that doesn't mean you'll
fly. If longevity is the
measure, why not be a
Hindu? They've got us beat
by fifteen hundred years.

MARTIN

Maybe. But no matter what
you say, I am a Catholic.
Some people have the
Harvard Club to drop into, I
have the church. Whether
I'm in Harlem, Prague, or
San Luis Obispo, I've always
got a church to visit.
Because whether you like it
or not, I am still a Catholic.

SISTER
CATHERINE
IMELDA

A very odd sort of Catholic.

MARTIN

Catholic. Catholic. Catholic.
That's what the word
means. You can't exclude
me. I can't exclude you.
Brian, on the other hand,
you, sir, are a pagan baby.

BRIAN

(*Still bagging but more slowly*) No, I'm a catechumen.

SISTER
CATHERINE
IMELDA

Of course, you are.

MARTIN

Maybe in your head, but not in your blood, Brian of the blessed baggies. One of the truths my mother never let me forget: Our people died for the right to call themselves Catholic. Yours didn't.

SISTER
CATHERINE
IMELDA

So, now you're preaching for the dying too? Fine. So, what are your thoughts on the afterlife? Enlighten the class.

MARTIN

The afterlife? (*Bagging again but slowly*) I suppose it's something that goes on and on and on — like filling these baggies. (Pauses and stares hard at her) But I

remember your views,
Sister. You once told my
mother that she would go to
hell. Without a doubt. With
no shot at redemption.

BRIAN stops his work

> SISTER
> CATHERINE
> IMELDA

I have no memory of that.

> MARTIN

No? Next stop, Hell, Mrs.
Mahoney. The Infernal pit.
The dark city, all burning
with brimstone and stinking
pitch, where the cries of its
many, many, many
inhabitants will send blood
gushing from your ears. No,
you didn't say all of that. Too
flowery for a straight
shooter like you. Just "You'll
go to hell, Mrs. Mahoney.
Mark my words." That's
what you said to my mother.
I was thirteen. There was no
need to elaborate on the
plunge into the infernal
abyss because she was a
good Irish lass, born in the
old country, where this
ridiculous shit was stirred

into their tea. But you made
Hell a personal passion for
me because, try as I might, I
could not get my mother to
shake it. You made your
mark: Give the devil her due.

BRIAN

I thought Hell was just a
case of not being with God.

MARTIN

They're keeping secrets
from you, Brian, me boy. For
the record, I added the
blood gushing out of the
ears part. Poetic license.

BRIAN

(Upset) Is this some sort of a
practical joke, his showing
up here, Sister? Is this a test?

MARTIN

I told you: Catholic college
before the seventies. Like
gasoline before they took
the lead out.

BRIAN

Sister? Did you tell his
mother she was going to
hell?

SISTER
CATHERINE
IMELDA

I cannot remember. *(Pause)*
It's not impossible. Taking
vows doesn't make you one
of the angels. Or Wonder
Woman. Teaching drove me
to despair.

MARTIN

The one unforgivable sin.

BRIAN

Nothing is unforgivable.
*(They both look at him, and
then SISTER laughs)*

SISTER
CATHERINE
IMELDA

Well... Anyway, another
sister introduced me to the
dry martini. One is not
enough and three is too
many.

MARTIN

Your memory is pretty selective, isn't it, Sister? I mean, you can remember the day you went into the convent and the nun who quit the Church to marry a Jewish shrink, but you don't remember my mother or me?

SISTER CATHERINE IMELDA

You all want to be remembered, as if I could dredge up every smirking face on demand. You want the indelible image of the acne-plagued thirteen-year-old with the gap tooth sitting in the third row to pop out of my head, so that we can all have a joyous reunion. But I remember none of you. Not even the ones I might have liked.

MARTIN

But you remember your despair.

SISTER
CATHERINE
IMELDA

I remember being weary,
yes. Hopeless. But not who
was there in the room while
I was despairing. That's the
evil of despair: being
trapped inside your own
mind. Forever.

MARTIN

And this was after taking
your vows?

SISTER
CATHERINE
IMELDA

I told you: The religious are
not immune to doubt.

BRIAN

We are all human.

MARTIN

Hold that thought. (*Back to
SISTER*) With that
experience, you still urge
him to give away fifty
million dollars and become a
monk.? Because being a
religious worked out so well
for you?

99

SISTER
CATHERINE
IMELDA

Brian has free will. We all
do.

MARTIN

And the despair disappears
by your being buddy-buddy
with the poor?

SISTER
CATHERINE
IMELDA

I'm not buddies with
anyone. Jesus said that you
had to feed the poor. He
didn't say you had to like
them. (*Beat*) I read that
somewhere.

MARTIN

(*To BRIAN*) Did you catch
the part about her vocation
leading to despair? Not a
surprise, given that this
team you're so eager to join
— the official Church — has
been in a pretty bad slump
lately. Recruiting violations,
you might call it.

SISTER
CATHERINE
IMELDA

I wondered when you would
finally get around to that.
Like clockwork. Why can't
you just leave him alone?
(*To BRIAN*) I think we have
enough. Wrap these up and
let's pack the car.

MARTIN

Have you kept him in a news
blackout about priests and
brothers who raped
children?

SISTER
CATHERINE
IMELDA

Every barrel has a few bad
apples. The good
outnumbered the bad one
hundred to one.

MARTIN

A few bad apples? More like
a plague of sex-starved
locusts. Night of the Living
Pedophiles. Actually, Night
after Night after Night of the
Living Pedophiles.

101

BRIAN

The scandals of the Church
are not a secret. They're
right out there for all to see.

MARTIN

Sure, now, when the Church
has no choice. But back then,
before the press got
interested, when the going
got tough, the whole team –
from Padua to Pittsburgh —
closed ranks.

BRIAN

I know about (*Beat*) that
stuff. My teachers have
explained all the ways the
Church has been hurt in its
history by some bad apples,
as Sister says.

MARTIN

All the ways? The whole
history? From the crusades
and inquisitions and
institutional anti-Semitism
to fighting birth control for
those same poor souls you
love so much?

SISTER
CATHERINE
IMELDA

You exaggerate.

102

MARTIN

(*To SISTER*) The Church
banned the waltz! What the
fuck was wrong with
dancing? (*BRIAN, horrified,
nevertheless keeps packing
boxes*)

SISTER
CATHERINE
IMELDA

The waltz? That's a new one
on me. But the church
changes. Anything created
by humans can make
mistakes. There was only
one perfect man — and they
crucified him.

MARTIN

You're repeating yourself.

SISTER
CATHERINE
IMELDA

(*Snorts*) What are you here
for? An apology?

MARTIN

No, I'm simply here to drop
off some toiletries. But God's
will be done: we meet.

(*Takes another bill out and slaps it on the table*) Here's a dollar. A hundred pennies for your thoughts, Sister. How is it that I can recite word for word that "Marriage is sacred" speech you made to my mother, but you draw a blank? Were we the start of your mission to the poor? Because we didn't have two dimes to rub together, thanks to the old man's benders. That apartment had thin walls, Sister. I heard it all. There was only one perfect man. Right? That was your idea of comforting. The husband is the head of the family -- for good or ill. That was your idea of counseling. All of us are free to make choices *but* if you choose divorce you will be damned for all eternity. You got right up close as you peddled that crap, right next to that line of bruises on her chin. Remember? She should have cracked your skull, but she couldn't lift her arm above her head. Not that afternoon. It was two years before I got big enough to toss his sorry ass down the stairs. Two long years. That

was one-hundred-and-four
weeks; front row seats in
the Fifth Circle of hell.

BRIAN

Why did your mother have
bruises? (*SISTER and
MARTIN both look at BRIAN*)

MARTIN

She walked into the kitchen
door. Twenty-seven times.

SISTER
CATHERINE
IMELDA

Too long ago to remember.
(*SISTER rises slowly with
another box*) What's done is
done. (*She exits through the
door to the outside*)

BRIAN

What is going on? Did Sister
do something to your
mother?

MARTIN

I have an idea for an app and
I'm gonna let you have it for
free. Next time, write an
algorithm that helps people
to find the nose on their

105

fucking face. (*Starts cleaning up manically*)

BRIAN

Sorry. Sorry. This is the most intense Midnight Run ever. Usually, we tell jokes while we fill the bags.

MARTIN

Fine. Heard the one about the guy who drops off a bunch of shampoo bottles in a church basement but finds the nun who fifty years earlier browbeat his poor mother into sticking around for the daily marital shellacking and … AND … a Ding-Dong who is giving away fifty million simoleons, so he can be a monk?

BRIAN

Your mother was a victim of domestic violence?

MARTIN

Domestic violence? Fuck that. She was a punching bag. And the whole parish knew it. Just like they knew who went to the country on vacation but really had a baby. And which altar boy was being diddled by the

cool "hoodlum priest" after basketball practice. And who drank and who stank and who sat around and gossiped about everyone else. And she — Sister Catherine Imelda of the Most Seraphic Baggie Ecstasies -- she knew it all. And she remembers.
(*Walking over to Brian*)
Which is why you should not let her talk you into this monastic fiasco.

BRIAN

You think Sister is talking me into becoming a monk? (*Laughs*) You've got it backwards. That decision was made before I met her. She tried to talk me out of it. Hustled me into this work to reflect. More than once, she's asked me if I am sure, but I stuck to it. She wants me to slow it down, but this is my passion, my grace, my gift from the Holy Spirit.

MARTIN

A gift. Okay, but why the Catholic Church? Why

107

become a monk? Isn't there still a Peace Corps out there? Doctors without Borders? Osteopaths Without Perimeters? Has the French Foreign Legion closed up shop?

BRIAN

Why is wanting to lead a holy life so absurd to everyone?

MARTIN

Absurd? No, absurd is being a Knicks fan or serving on the architectural review board in Cherry Hill, New Jersey. A youthful genius hiding away in a monastery: that's a complete waste. You don't know what the Church can be like. Study its magnificent stupidity and casual cruelty for a few years.

BRIAN

Choosing this life for myself wasn't easy. Try telling your agnostic, Liberal Democrat, National Public Radio, Charter Planned Parenthood Member aunts that the next step in your life is entering a life of solitude and service in

an abbey and see what
happens.

MARTIN

My aunts would eat your
aunts for breakfast: bones
and all. What about the rest
of us? Maybe we need you
here in this world making
mystical algorithms to tell
us what to do so we don't
blow up the planet.

*SISTER re-enters quietly and
busies herself with throwing out
the empty bags from the food*

BRIAN

With a software developer's
shopping algorithm? I don't
think so.

MARTIN

Do software developers take
a vow of celibacy?

BRIAN

(*Pause*) Of course. That was
Wozniak's idea.

MARTIN

Really?

BRIAN

Ha! No. Ha! That was a joke.
(*Notices SISTER off to the*

side) See? We still can have fun doing this. Not a night of "uninterrupted hilarity," but fun.

MARTIN

And being a monk in a church filled with all sorts of obsessive rules? If that sounds like fun to you, the vow of celibacy is redundant.

SISTER
CATHERINE
IMELDA

Brian wants a life of charity. No one does more charity than the Church. Even if they did ban the waltz.

MARTIN

So, go do Charity! Drop everything and do Charity now. You hustle out there with that fifty million dollars and get cracking.

BRIAN

I am doing it now. Packing
up is what we are supposed
to be doing now. Not
debating my vocation.

SISTER
CATHERINE
IMELDA

(*To MARTIN*) At least, he
wants to be a Catholic. You
remember being a Catholic
before you left the 'official'
church?

MARTIN

I never left. I'm Catholic, but
I'm in the resistance. And
our side's winning. Walk
into any church on Sunday:
you can have your pick of
empty pews. The rest of us
are voting with our knees.
You said you were a dying
breed, right? Well, well
what's keeping you?
Because when you all die off,
we'll start over with more
feasts than fasting, more
healing than hellfire. More
midnight mass than messing
with other people's lives. So,
feel free to die anytime.

BRIAN

That's a terrible thing to say.
Horrible. I don't know
whether you're joking or
not.

MARTIN

Neither do I. But at least I
didn't trot out a few lines
from scripture and condemn
her to the eternal fires of
hell.

BRIAN

Would you regret that
incident now, Sister? If you
remembered it?

SISTER
CATHERINE
IMELDA

That's between me and God.

BRIAN

Of course.

MARTIN

And my mother, who has
more of an in with God than
you do these days. What
with being dead and all.

BRIAN

Just stop. Lay off. Sister does
so much for other people.
The woman is a saint.

SISTER
CATHERINE
IMELDA

No saints here, Brian.

MARTIN

No, you're right; she's a
saint. And you can be her
disciple. Blessed Brian of
Bedford Hills.

BRIAN

What have you got against
me, Martin? I'm just trying
to get closer to God, that's
all. Is that a crime? Aren't we
supposed to want to be
more than we are?

MARTIN

No, that's the United States
Army recruiting motto.
Okay, if you've got your
heart set on it, go ahead and
be more divine. But why
does everyone on your quest
have to leave this world
behind? (*MARTIN advances
on BRIAN*)

BRIAN

We're helping the poor
tonight.

MARTIN

Oh, please! You're giving
them shampoo and crackers
and then you're driving back
to Westchester.

BRIAN

Connecticut.

MARTIN

Why do you need to go away
and live in a damp, dark,
dank cell in order to be
holy? Why separate yourself
from the real pain people
suffer? All you're doing is
making a separate peace.

BRIAN

I just want to get away from
myself and lose myself in
God. That's all.

SISTER
CATHERINE
IMELDA

Brian, a vocation is not a
vacation from who we are.
It's a ... struggle. Listening,
waiting, working,

contemplating. With no
guarantee of ever finding
God.

MARTIN

A struggle. So, we finally
agree on something.

BRIAN

(*Thoroughly exasperated*)
You honestly think I don't
know that?

MARTIN AND
SISTER
CATHERINE
IMELDA

Yes. (*They look at each other
with surprise*)

SISTER
CATHERINE
IMELDA

No. Forgive me. (*She walks
slowly over to a chair and
sinks into it*) It's
complicated.

MARTIN

The real saints are in the
world.

SISTER
CATHERINE
IMELDA

(*Turning on him with a fury*)
Lapsed Catholics know
everything and believe
nothing. Now you're an
expert on the saints?

MARTIN

(*In her face shouting*) Just
like you were an expert on
marriage.

BRIAN

Stop yelling! Both of you.
This...this is why people
have so much trouble with
Catholics. You're too intense.

MARTIN

Maybe that's because we
were all taught by people
who never got laid.

BRIAN

(*Standing up to MARTIN's
more insistent posture*) You
can't say this kind of stuff to
Sister.

SISTER
CATHERINE
IMELDA

Don't take the bait, Brian.

BRIAN

And your Catholic schooling
should have taught you that
chastity offers strength to
avoid getting sidetracked on
the way to perfect love, to
experience heaven while on
earth.

MARTIN

Sex isn't getting sidetracked.
It's the main event.

SISTER
CATHERINE
IMELDA

You're the very devil. Let
him be.

BRIAN

(*Almost reciting*)
'Distractions of everyday life
block the path toward
holiness.' Distractions like
you, Martin. (*More agitated*)
And what could be more
ordinary than having sex?
Everybody has sex. Not
everybody can be a monk —
realizing a union with God,
Christ, the Church, the
Mystical Body — that's
extraordinary! And no
matter what you or anyone
else says I'm super-focused
— super focused on...//

MARTIN

Holiness isn't hiding. (*Points to SISTER*) Even she admits that. Don't hide from life, grab it, kiss it, and make something out of it before you're too old and washed up. Every piece, every act. (*In BRIAN's face*) Breathing is holy, right? You were a Buddhist. Sleeping is holy. Dalai Lama, "Sleep: most important form of meditation." (*Picks up some crackers*) Eating is holy, "The Son of Man came eating and drinking." Matthew 11:19 (*SISTER picks up the broom unbeknownst to Martin.*) Come on, taste that. peanut butter. (*Shoves a cracker in BRIAN's mouth while he tries to break free*) Nectar of the gods. Holy.

Sister pushes the head of broom
repeatedly at Martin's back

SISTER
CATHERINE
IMELDA

Martin Mahoney! (*She*
connects several times until
the broom drops from her
hands.) Leave the poor man
alone!

MARTIN wheels around and is
almost chin to chin with SISTER,
but he walks away just as BRIAN
is about to block him

MARTIN

(*Over his shoulder*) You
remembered my name.

BRIAN

What just happened? This is
not supposed to happen
here. We are in Church.

MARTIN

It's the basement.

BRIAN

Seriously, what kind of
Catholics are you?

119

SISTER retreats to a chair in
silence

                    MARTIN

Cradle.

                    BRIAN

Crazy Catholics! Crazy! What
was that?

                    MARTIN

Just like the good old days,
Sister. (*Picks up the broom*)
Couldn't find your trusty
steel ruler? (*SISTER laughs*)

                         SISTER
                         CATHERINE
                         IMELDA

(*Points to the crumbs on the*
floor) Put in a dollar for
those crackers. (*Martin*
laughs and does so.)

                    BRIAN

What's so funny?

                    MARTIN

You've just witnessed Sister
administering my
mortification of the flesh.
With a broom!

SISTER
CATHERINE
IMELDA

Mortification! Such
nonsense. That's not what
Christ wants.

BRIAN

(*Dusting off crumbs*) Well, I
don't think he wants peanut
butter crackers for
communion either.

SISTER
CATHERINE
IMELDA

(*To MARTIN*) More sacrilege.
You're a real piece of work.
A Catholic education and
here you are browbeating
him for wanting a vocation.

BRIAN

This is all so confusing to
me.

SISTER
CATHERINE
IMELDA

Life is confusing.

BRIAN

But that's why I joined the
church! Ten years hanging
out with people who act as if
God is the phone in their
pocket. Who obsess about
knowing where we have
been and where we are
going, the ways our eyes
dilate when we see someone
we like, how our body
temperature rises. I just
want to be a monk and get
closer to God. Why is that so
hard to understand? You're
Catholic. You're a nun. He's
…

MARTIN

An ex-beat writer for the
Mets and Jets. Which some
observers have called the
work of Satan.

SISTER
CATHERINE
IMELDA

Don't blame sports writing
on the Devil. (*To BRIAN*) I
almost wish you weren't so
sure about your calling,
Brian. Presumption…//

BRIAN

(*Interrupting*) You're repeating yourself, Sister.

SISTER
CATHERINE
IMELDA

(*Pointing to her veil*) That's all this life is, Brian. Endless repetition. Are you ready for that?

BRIAN

Why does everyone keep asking me if I'm ready? People go to Burning Man every year and make fools of themselves. Perfectly acceptable, makes the *Times* Style section. But I state that my belief that God's will is for me to become a monk and my mental health gets called into question. Idiots devote their entire existence to trying to be on *American Idol*. Fine. They spend every waking hour making stupid YouTube videos about their cats. That's cool. A whole cabal of so-called human beings say the same moronic things night after night on cable news and we don't question their sanity.

MARTIN

Actually, we do question their sanity. Especially the ones on Fox.

BRIAN

People are complete assholes to everyone around them and make themselves hideously rich, but we say those guys are just fine. Why not go and give them a hard time?

MARTIN

Brian, if they came in here, no matter how many tiny bottles of conditioners they had, I would totally bust their balls. I would. Even if they had the even higher-quality Seven-Grain Sea Salt crackers. Honest. But in this church basement right now, I work with the squad provided — including a multi-millionaire algorithm spinner.

BRIAN

(*Sneeringly*) Algorithms are nothing but complex rules. Rules. The things you dismiss and detest.

MARTIN

Not all rules: just the tiny, bullshit, niggling, mess-with-your life rules. "Woe to you, scribes and Pharisees, hypocrites!"

BRIAN

Stop it! Being Catholic is not some sort of *American Gladiators* Bible-thumping contest. You don't care about what happens to me or Sister or anybody else. You're a burnout with a grudge against the Church and Sister Catherine. You're a hypocrite.

MARTIN

That doesn't change the fact that an inventor of a top-notch, fifty-million-dollar predictive algorithm shouldn't waste his life…//

BRIAN

What do you even know about algorithms? Do you even know how the internet works? You ought to by now; Twitter and Facebook probably took your sports

writing job. Here's a
suggestion: Try actually
reading some social media.
Because when you do, you'll
be chasing me down to
apologize for even
suggesting that I should go
back to being one of the
masters of a universe filled
with Jihadists, Nazis, Antifas,
incels, and venture
capitalists.

SISTER
CATHERINE
IMELDA

For what doth it profit a
man, if he gain the whole
world and lose his own soul?
(*Martin opens his mouth to
speak but stops.*)

BRIAN

Or make other people lose
their souls. What I did, what
I would do if I went back, is
to just be another player in
the game.

MARTIN

Winner of the game.

BRIAN

(*Agitated*) I'm a coder, not a
crusader. Pay attention. I

126

was an online sleepwalking
series of numbers. But I
woke up. I looked at Sikh
and Sufi and Baha'i. I went
to a Zoroastrian
informational session! And I
ended up with Christ.

MARTIN

For now. But like any other
die-hard hobbyist, for you
temptation is always lurking
in the next catalogue. Maybe
space age religion is in your
future, worshipping at the
House of Retz in Venus. Or
just hot Zen yoga.

BRIAN

(*Fiercer*) I have faith in Jesus
Christ, my Lord and Savior,
Martin. What do you have?
Cynicism and jokes. My faith
gives me peace. Being a real
Catholic is being special.

SISTER
CATHERINE
IMELDA

Oh, dear Lord, Brian,
wanting to be special is so
ordinary. Wanting is the
trouble. Wanting to help.

127

Wanting to be holy. You have to seek without wanting. This closeness to God — it's not certain. No matter how much you pray, no matter how deep you dig into your cell, you might only find questions. You wait and wait and the whole world seems to be saying no to you every morning, noon, and night, a "no" that only you can hear.

BRIAN

It's not going to be that way for me, Sister. The Catholic Church is my big Yes. Yes. Yes. It's the end of my chain of reasoning, so I don't have to reason anymore. If this, then that. (*To MARTIN*) That's a really mystical algorithm.

MARTIN

(*Pedantically*) A mystical predictive algorithm?

SISTER
CATHERINE
IMELDA

You'll kill us with your
cuteness.

BRIAN

He's not cute! (*Gradually
yelling louder and louder at
MARTIN*) You call yourself
Catholic? Then what about
"lifting up your heart" the
way we all do in Church on
Sunday? Tried that recently?
Of course, you haven't.
You're sad. You're bitter.
And I am... (*Throws his
baggies violently into an
empty box*) Happy. Content.
Focused. Blessed. (*Realizes
how loud he is and pauses
before continuing in a
calmer, lower tone*) You're
too afraid to believe, too
worried about what the big
bad church is going to do to
you. I have passion. I have
hope. What do you have?

SISTER
CATHERINE
IMELDA

(*To BRIAN*) Passion fades.
No shortcuts to Paradise.
But we may need a shortcut
to The Bronx at this hour.
Our recipients will be
waiting. (*Stands*) Let's get
the rest of this stuff into the
car.

BRIAN

I'll do it. Anything to escape.
(*Leaves with boxes*)

MARTIN

No doubts about what Brian
is doing?

SISTER
CATHERINE
IMELDA

I keep my doubts to myself.
Maybe Brian is God's fool,

MARTIN

But don't you think you
should stop him before he

gives away fifty million? He could wake up one morning in the Abbey looking for his wallet.

SISTER
CATHERINE
IMELDA

Can't tell people what to do. This is that for which he was created. He was made to be blessed. Or broken.

MARTIN

And for what were you created, Sister?

SISTER
CATHERINE
IMELDA

Not for much, it turns out. Not for teaching wiseacres too smart for their own good. And not for telling people what to do. Not for promising damnation to a woman looking to run away from a vicious drunk. I was twenty-five. Twenty-five. I had no business giving anyone advice about anything. I was out of my depth, quoting the party

line. Because I was twenty-
five. (She hesitates.)
Damnation. (*Shakes head*)
Your mother was lovely.
Lovely woman. *Mea culpa.
Mea culpa. Mea maxima
culpa.*

MARTIN

I thought you only confessed
to God.

SISTER

CATHERINE

IMELDA

There's a big difference
between a story and a
confession.

MARTIN

Not in my line of work. So,
what's your story?

SISTER CATHERINE IMELDA

Do you remember Sister
John Laurentia? Mother
Superior in our convent?
(*MARTIN shakes his head.*)
You could have missed her,
but she did not miss a thing.
God bless her. She saw what
an abomination I was in the
classroom — and
everywhere else. "Go out
and help the poor," she said.
That old woman looked
inside me, saw how lost I
was. "Go help the poor,
Catherine", she said. Go help
the poor. But in my
presumption, I said "Why?
Why?" Mother smiled at me.
She quoted a poet priest, a
Jesuit — Hopkins. A friend
had asked him how he might
believe in God, and Hopkins
simply said, "Give alms."
Took me much longer to
figure that out.

MARTIN

How long?

SISTER
CATHERINE
IMELDA

Forever. (*Beat*) Touch the
poor. Yes, touch them. Talk
to them again and again. Not
because that's where God is
or that's what Christ said,
but because that's the only
way you can let go of this all-
consuming desire to know
everything. It's an awful
burden, isn't it? Needing to
have all the answers. The
poor have no time for that
nonsense. (*BRIAN returns,
and she touches his shoulder*)
Nor do the Blessed.

BRIAN

I'm really sorry. Actually, I'm
sorry for you guys and for
what you're going through.
And I'm sorry for what you
put me through too —but—I
can't go tonight. I just can't.

SISTER
CATHERINE
IMELDA

Oh, Brian.

BRIAN

No, it's all good. Well, no, it's
not. I can't go down there
angry and help people.
Garbage in. Garbage out. I'm
better off just praying and
being alone with God.

MARTIN

Hang on a second. (*Grabbing
another package of crackers,
opens it, and starts to eat
while sticking a dollar bill in
SISTER's pocket*) Who's
going to drive her car to The
Bronx?

SISTER
CATHERINE
IMELDA

The good Lord will provide.
He always does. And He will
be there for you too, Brian.
You don't need to chase Him
so hard. But let's say a
prayer together before you
go. If only to calm the
waters.

BRIAN

What are we praying for?

MARTIN

Dying breeds.

135

                    SISTER
                    CATHERINE
                    IMELDA

        Our Father...

*BRIAN reflexively seeks to hold
hands with MARTIN who demurs
and then relents*

                    MARTIN

        Is this the Anointing of the
        Sick, Brian?

                    BRIAN

        (They pick up again) Our
        Father…

                    SISTER & BRIAN

        Who art in Heaven
        Hallowed be thy name
        thy Kingdom Come, thy will
        be done on Earth as it is in
        Heaven. Give us this day our
        daily bread

*MARTIN deliberately swallows
his cracker and joins in*

                    SISTER & BRIAN
                    & MARTIN

        And forgive us our
        trespasses (*SISTER gestures
        to Martin at this*)

SISTER
CATHERINE
IMELDA

(*Emphatically*) And forgive us our trespasses as we forgive those who trespass against us.

MARTIN

(*Spouting crumbs*) Who is forgiving whom here?

SISTER
CATHERINE
IMELDA

Jesus says to forgive someone who has wronged you "not seven times but seventy times seven".

MARTIN

Matthew 6 Verses 9-11.

BRIAN

Stop!

SISTER
CATHERINE
IMELDA

I forgive you.

MARTIN

You forgive me?

SISTER
CATHERINE
IMELDA

I forgive you your trespasses
and you forgive me my
trespasses.

MARTIN

Trespasses? Hey, I'm the guy
who dropped off the extra-
dry conditioner.

SISTER
CATHERINE
IMELDA

I forgive you for making me
remember.

BRIAN

(*Impatient*) And lead us...

MARTIN

You forgive me?

SISTER
CATHERINE
IMELDA

Who ever said Catholicism
was fair? So, you forgive me
for your mother. I hope so,
at least. (*MARTIN turns his
head from her*) That's why
they call it a prayer.

BRIAN

And lead us not into temptation but deliver us from evil. (Sister catches up to him and all again pray together) For thine is the power and the glory ...//

MARTIN

(*Turning back*) In Luke Chapter 18, Jesus does give the team that pep talk about praying always and not to lose heart. But I'm forgiving you?

BRIAN

That's it. I'm out of here. (*To SISTER*) Sorry. (*To MARTIN*) Not sorry. Coders know when to exit. (*Heads to door hands in air*)

MARTIN

Dominus vobiscum. Vaya con dios. Cheerio!

SISTER
CATHERINE
IMELDA

(*SISTER tries to stop him but he brushes by her*) Brian. I will call you. (*She picks up one last box*)

MARTIN

See you in Church.

BRIAN

God, I hope not. (*He leaves*)

SISTER
CATHERINE
IMELDA

Well, now I need a driver,
Mister Mahoney. Yes, you.
Even a lapsed Catholic will
do, as long as he has a valid
driver's license. You're
coming with me to The
Bronx. If only to help me
explain these horrible
baggies. Even the poor have
standards.

MARTIN

I only came here to drop off
toiletries.

SISTER
CATHERINE
IMELDA

Come. Just do. Remember?
To be is to do. Do be do be
doo.

MARTIN

Remembering is not one of
my problems.

                    SISTER
                    CATHERINE
                    IMELDA

Give alms. Feed the poor.
See God. It's a package deal,
Martin. "Water quenches a
flaming fire, and alms atone
sins."

                    MARTIN

(*Resists the urge to give the
reference*) Rita will be
waiting.

                    SISTER
                    CATHERINE
                    IMELDA

Lucky man that you are. But
it was her suggestion that
you come here tonight. And
then, Mirabile Dictu, you got
conscripted into the Army of
the Lord. For a few hours.
Just a few. You'll be back by
two. She'll forgive you. She
will.

*MARTIN stands still. SISTER
heads out the door. He hesitates,
then grabs the last box and
follows*

                    MARTIN

Jesus, Mary, and Joseph.

END OF
PLAY

Milton Keynes UK
Ingram Content Group UK Ltd.
UKHW051452140724
445326UK00013BA/514